slumber kins®

This book belongs to

Scan here for additional resources and digital content for Slumberkins' books.

slumberkins®

LEARN

How To BEE Helpful

By Kelly Oriard with Callie Christensen

Illustrated by Noona Vinogradoff

Deep in the woods
five friends sat to play,
laughing, and snacking,
and gabbing away.

Just then,
little Ibex sat up with a start,
feeling a pain
inside of his heart.

1

"Something is wrong,"
said Ibex with fear,
"I know it inside me,
the feeling is clear."

All of the creatures
sat up to attend
the message from Ibex,
their sensitive friend.

"Yes, I feel it, I feel it,
it's getting quite strong;
the woods are unhappy,
and something is wrong!"

Just then, Honey Bee traveled
near the young crew,
sniffling and crying sad tears
as she flew.

2

"What's wrong little friend?"
Ibex said, full of care,
"Why the sad face and the tears
— will you share?"

Honey Bee took a breath
and she calmed herself down,

"MY HOME
IS DESTROYED,"

she said with a frown.

3

The thing about Ibex
we should all learn to see:
Ibex knows from the heart
if things aren't as they should be.

We can *all* be like Ibex
when something is wrong,
check in with our hearts,
it shouldn't take long.

4

"Oh no!" Yeti cried
without missing a beat.
"We must fix your home,"
and she jumped to her feet.

As Yeti took off
to find Honey Bee's home,
Honey Bee sat there,
confused and alone.

Where's Yeti going?
She doesn't yet know
that the problem is bigger
and starting to grow.

Before you get up
and set out on your task,
be mindful and slow down,
and be sure to ask.

5

The friends all called out
to their dear Yeti kin,
"Slow down and come back,
let us learn and check in.

We love your fast pace
and your big open heart,
but be mindful and calm down,
begin at the start."

Yeti came back
and she slowed herself down;
sitting, and breathing,
and looking around.

"I'll learn to check in
with my friend like I should—
because rushing ahead
can cause more harm than good."

The friends sat together
to inquire some more,
and Honey Bee shared
the challenge in store.

"I do want your help,
but the problem is big—

My hive fell to the ground
and it snapped from a twig."

"My family is homeless
and needing some aid,
it's not just our branch
where the problem's been mad

"The whole forest is sick
and grows weaker by day.
What is the problem?
I wish I could say."

7

Honey Bear listened,
feeling grateful Honey Bee shared,
then wondered aloud, how to support those
who feel scared.

"There are lots of big problems
for us to address.
What can we do
that will help out the best?"

The friends sat together,
all feeling confused.
Honey Bear turned to Bee asking,
"What do you think we should do?"

Bee replied,
because she'd given some thought,

"LET'S SEARCH
ALL TOGETHER FOR
THE SOURCE OF
THE ROT."

Honey Bear had
some great thoughts on this day,
to help out the bees
in the very best way.

It's important to ask
how and where we should start.
We can all work together,
each doing our part.

The friends all agreed,
and the Honey Bee too,
they took off in search
of the good they could do.

The friends traveled far,
as trees withered away,
and they ended their mission
down by the bay.

They stood at the edge,
feeling shock and surprise.
The gray and brown water
brought tears to their eyes.

The town had been dumping
old berries in there,
rotting and spoiling
the water and air.

11

The air was polluted
and so were the trees.
This must be the source
of what's hurting the bees!

When the Earth has been hurt,
we all feel hurt too.
The friends knew at once
what they all had to do.

12

They started right up,
with a well thought out plan,
knowing they must fix
both water and land.

"We must clean the forest,
the water and kelp.
We'll go into town
and ask others for help!"

They requested permission
to help their dear friends,
and told the town leaders
the pollution must end.

"We must stop this dumping
of berries, of course.
This problem will end
if it's stopped at the source."

14

They all worked together,
to clean up the space,
cleaning and running
all over the place.

Out to the water,
to pick berries up at the shore.
Back to the forest, fixing twigs,
branches, and more.

15

Feeling tired, exhausted,
they started to slow,
but knowing the importance,
they continued to go.

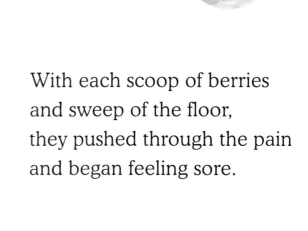

With each scoop of berries
and sweep of the floor,
they pushed through the pain
and began feeling sore.

16

Slumber Sloth noticed
his friends needed a break.
They'd forgotten themselves
while cleaning the lake.

He knew the importance
of finding some time
to take care of yourself,
to be at your prime.

He called to his friends, "IT'S TIME FOR A SIT- LET'S REST FOR A MINUTE, AND EAT FOR A BIT."

18

The group all sat down,
including the bees,
snacking, and talking,
and leaning on trees.

19

When working to help,
remember self-care.
We can solve problems better
when we come up for air.

Slumber Sloth checked in with himself
and his body did know—
our own needs are important
when we're on the go.

After the break,
the friends cleaned up some more—
they felt proud of themselves
as they sat on the shore.

They'd all worked together
to help out the bees
who'd rebuilt their homes
in much cleaner trees.

The bees felt grateful
for the help they received,
thanking their friends
for all they achieved.

Otter began
to reflect on the day,
realizing the importance
of helping in a respectful way.

They stood alongside
their friends, the honeybees,
helping to make a plan
to fix up the trees.

They got permission to help,
and others joined too,
all working together:
a big caring crew!

They stood with bees,
in their big time of need.
They listened, worked hard,
and completed the deed.

22

They didn't ask to be heroes,
or get lots of praise,
they helped heal the Earth
in the kindest of ways.

Now the honeybees
had a safe place to live,
the friends realized
they had so much to give.

Together we all live
and breathe the same air,
and taking care of our Earth
shows that we all care.

"It feels good to be helpers,"
Otter said from the shade,
"But what feels even better
are the friends that we've made."

The bees buzzed around,
and the friends all agreed,
they had learned about helping
and caring, indeed.

The lesson was clear
what they learned on this day.
They said it out loud
to remember the way:

When I feel something is wrong
I can ask where to start.
Helping others in need,
together each doing our part.

About the Authors:

Co-authors Kelly Oriard and Callie Christensen saw a need for intentional social-emotional resources for young children and founded Slumberkins in 2016. Kelly is a skilled family therapist and licensed school counselor. Callie is a licensed elementary and special education teacher. Kelly and Callie have been best friends for more than 20 years and live in the Pacific Northwest with their families.

Learn more about the authors and Slumberkins at www.slumberkins.com.

slumber kins ®

Slumberkins designs approachable tools that promote early emotional learning. Our stories use research-based techniques to teach important social-emotional skills while deepening the parent-child bond.

The Slumberkins family of creatures includes:

 SLUMBER SLOTH
relaxation

 YETI
mindfulness

 ALPACA
stress relief

 BIGFOOT
self-esteem

 OTTER
family bonding

 SPRITE
grief & loss

 FOX
family change

 NARWHAL
growth mindset

 THE FEELS
emotional well-being

 HAMMERHEAD
conflict resolution

 UNICORN
authenticity

 HONEY BEAR
gratitude

 IBEX
emotional courage

 LYNX
self-expression

 YAK
self-acceptance